# DOLLY

In sinful collaboration with the enticing Princess Dolly.

**Some parts of this book are based on true events.**

But there is only one way to find out which ones.

Follow @princess.dolly on OF

For all those good Catholic girls who spent
every Sunday on their knees.
You know who you are.
You've been a good girl, this one's for you.

# I.

Samuel Russo stood at the pulpit looking out over the nave. It was early morning and the church was still empty. He gently touched his stole, his fingers caressing the fabric softly as he tried to sooth the butterflies in his stomach.

He felt nauseous and his breath was unsteady. After years of studying and completing his time at the seminary, today would be his first day as a priest. He'd finished his time as a transitional deacon under the incredible Arch-Bishop Murray, a strict holy man with no room for nonsense. He was highly respected amongst everyone else called by God and he was beloved by his flock.

But now, his time with him had come to an end, and he'd finally taken up his own position as head of congregation.

He'd been called to a small township in the middle of England following the not-so-unexpected passing of Bishop Harrison who had run the congregation for well over 60 years. Samuel hadn't formally met any of the churchgoers yet and he was a mass on anxious nerves and hoping his apparent lack of experience by comparison wouldn't go against him.

He closed his eyes and whispered a silent prayer. God would look after him. He always had.

He took one final look around, taking everything in before heading to the entrance, ready to greet his new flock.

The sun was shining outside and it was a fresh spring morning - perfect for a new beginning.

Samuel greeted each person as they filed in, introducing himself politely and giving his commiserations for the loss of Bishop Harrison. He felt his nerves slowly settling, the anxiety filtering away with every new person he spoke to. He smiled to himself, everything was going to be fine, it was as God had intended.

He headed back to the pulpit ready to start his sermon. He'd prepared some wonderful passages about new beginnings, the start of spring and the welcoming of a new flock - combined with the beautiful day outside, everything felt like it was falling into place.
He began with a passage from Jeremiah 29:11, soothing confidence washing over him. He could feel his voice growing stronger as he stood taller, the powerful energy filling him as he spoke to the eager people before him. Everything was going according to plan-
And then she walked in.

The door opened with a small bang and the dull clack of heels could be heard on the flagstones. Samuel lost his place in his sermon for a second as he looked up. He saw a curvaceous blonde scuttle down the aisle. Her dress was short, scarcely covering her buttocks and her...chest-moved extensively as she searched for a seat. There was only a space on the front row, and blushing apologetically, she clambered over a few people to reach it. She gave an apologetic wave as she sat down. Samuel felt the need to drag his eyes away - in a room of modestly dressed and appropriate women, this one stood out. Was she in the right place? He tried desperately to banish her from his thoughts and push on with his sermon. He averted his eyes to an elderly couple holding hands on the opposite pew, banishing thoughts of the blond from his mind as he pushed through.

As the prayers and songs of praise continued, he found himself making a conscious effort not to look in her direction, the bright dress and abundance of skin were difficult to ignore. He made a mental note to discuss proper church attire - it was wholly inappropriate and clearly a distraction to other churchgoers.

"And I will give you a new heart and put a new spirit in you; I will remove from you your heart of stone and give you a heart of flesh." He spoke clearly and concluded his sermon, advising of a time for confessionals before the communion.

He regarded the congregation as people filtered out or queued up as he took his position in the confessional.

He listened carefully as each person filed in, confessing their sins.

He listened as they spoke about their immoral thoughts, that they had considered if God was truly there and he felt his heart heavy with the sadness of each admission - each sin. There was a scuffle outside the box and a small clatter. Samuel kept his eyes downcast as the voice filtered in,

"Bless me father for I have sinned, it has been one week since my last confessional."

"Tell me of your sins."

There was a brief pause. "Last night I met with a man in a nightclub, I had a couple of drinks, as you do. So I, like, went home with him... and his wife. He asked me to kiss his wife, and like, watched as I kissed her, touched her boobs and stuff. Can I say boobs in church?" She continued before he had a chance to speak, "He also told me to lick her...erm...pussy- sorry father, I don't know what else to call it. So anyway, I licked her until she came, because you know, that's what I'd been told to do, and then she played with my boobs whilst her husband fuc-had sex with me." There was a long pause, she seemed to be waiting for something.

Samuel sat for a moment, unsure how to respond. He knew what he needed to say but the shock of the confession sat with him for a moment. Had all of that really happened? He'd heard of affairs...but this was...interesting. He'd led a sheltered life and he felt the heat burn under his cheeks.

"I-is that everything, my child?"

"No."

Samuel swallowed. "Please, confess all of your sins." He closed his eyes and took a steadying breath.

"I confess to performing sexual acts on an online platform. I post videos where I touch myself, touch other women, get spat on and dance for other people's pleasure." There was a sigh, "I was also late for church this morning because I woke up at the home of the married couple from last night, and we had another round. Nothing as fun-erm-intense-erm...you know what I mean. Nothing like last night, but still some stuff, you know?"

Samuel could feel himself blushing, his cheeks hot under his skin. He took a steady breath - there was no doubt of who was in the box, he'd known the instant she began to speak - the voice matched so perfectly to her appearance. He cleared his mind of the creeping images in his mind, he knew he needed to offer advice, offer council- but he was unsure where to begin. He had left school and been called to God - he had sworn a vow of celibacy, and, as a virgin he felt especially called. He had no interest in flesh. And now, on the very first day, God had chosen to send him a test.

"And do you regret what happened?" There was a pause for thought -

"I do."

"And will you work to live in God's name and do good, and remove yourself from immorality?"

"I will."

"I forgive you, and so does God. Let us pray together. Repeat with me-My God, I am sorry for my sins with all my heart. In choosing to do wrong and failing to do good, I have sinned against You whom I should love above all things. I firmly intend, with Your help, to do penance, to sin no more, and to avoid whatever leads me to sin. Our Savior Jesus Christ suffered and died for us. In his name, my God, have mercy." He listened as the words echoed back.

"Thank you father...."

"Russo. Priest Russo."

"Thank you, I'm Dolly!"

"You do not need to give your name..." But it was too late, as he heard the gentle click of the door, he realized that she had already left.

Samuel sat in the dark of the confessional for a moment, his mind and heartbeat racing. This was normal. He reminded himself. People sin. God forgives. He whispered this to himself a few times over, but the mental image of the curvy blonde and the dress barely covering her thick thighs and...

No.

He swallowed. He was in church. He was a man of God. He had taken a vow. He closed his eyes again in silent prayers before stepping out of the box. He wondered if she was a regular at the church or had just stumbled across it. She certainly looked out of place. He resolved himself to have a discussion with her, should she return, about church-appropriate attire and offer the council that he felt unable to offer today.

# II.

The next Sunday rolled around and Samuel had had substantial difficulty keeping Dolly out of his mind. Were these the trials he was set to go through? Were these the temptations the devil would use? He needed to be strong. He needed focus and absolute dedication to his belief. He knew he could do this and cast aside the unholy thoughts.

This woman needed help.

Yes. That's right.

And it was his job as priest to support her, to help her recognise her life of sin, and lead her towards a more moral and holy path. She attended church - so surely she must be a follower of Christ.

Much like the week before he greeted each of his flock as they filtered through. The weather was bright and he was prepared should the curvaceous blonde return to his parish. As the line of worshippers filtered down, he was beginning to believe she wasn't showing up - perhaps it had been a one off. Just as he was about to turn and take his place at the front of the church he heard the unmistakable clatter of heels.

"Hi Priest Russo! I'm not too late this time am I?" He felt his jaw slacken for a moment before he closed his mouth firmly shut. Dolly was running up the path in high heels, a tight skirt hugging her thighs and a low, deep V blouse which tucked in at her waist. There was movement in her thighs and chest as she ran towards him, the cut of her shirt barely covering the flesh beneath.

He could see the outline of her stomach under the pencil skirt, the womanly softness restricted by the tight fabric-

No.

He cut his thoughts off. This was improper. He took a steady breath, flexing his hand over his trouser leg, praying the fabric would ground him.

"Dolly." He greeted her with a tight lipped smile.

"Hi! I am totally looking forward to your like, sermon thing today. Was thinking about everything you said last week about new beginnings and all of that, and like, I totally took it onboard."

He looked at her outfit, "Dolly...I need to talk to you." She smiled at him, he pressed on, "About your outfit. It isn't...appropriate for church. But I'm very glad you took onboard what I said last week."

"Oh no! Can you tell I don't have panties on?!" She looked shocked, "It's just, it's sooo nice out, and like, I can feel the sun through my skirt and it feels super good on my pussy - you know what I mean? But I totally get it, next week panties. I suppose God is watching!"

She pranced inside, leaving Samuel dumbstruck at the conversation.

He shook his head, hoping to shake the impure thoughts that were trying to enter. No panties. He swallowed, closing his eyes and clutching the rosary he kept in his pocket. Think of God.

Samuel took his place in the pulpit and began his service. No matter what he did, he found himself distracted, his eyes wandering to Dolly in the second row, her legs elegantly crossed. He watched as she fidgeted for a moment before uncrossing, and recrossing her legs. He faltered in his speech as his heart skipped a beat. The skirt was too tight for anything salacious to have been displayed, but despite this, he was drawn to her - a niggling, repressed thought crying out, wishing to have caught a glimpse.

He searched desperately for his place on the page, looking at his prepared notes, he fumbled again before finishing -

"And whatever you do, in word or deed, do everything in the name of the Lord Jesus, giving thanks to God the Father through him."

He closed his bible and closed his eyes for a few moments. He'd made it through. He turned to look at the beautiful stained windows.

*God. Please, banish these thoughts from my mind, lead me from this unholy temptation.*

He regained his composure and took his place in the confessional box again. At least there should be no Dolly - she said she'd taken everything onboard, that felt like a relief.

Samuel felt a sense of calm washing over him, he listened patiently through the minor sins of the week, reminding each person of God's love, of his forgiveness.

"Bless me father for I have sinned, it has been one week since my last confessional."

Shit. He heard the familiar voice. He kept his eyes downcast. Perhaps it wouldn't be so bad?

"Tell me of your sins." He closed his eyes, his hands grasping each other. *Please God, please do not test me. I feel weak and need your support and guidance...*

"I uploaded some videos to the internet." Oh. That

wasn't so bad, he let out a sigh.

"I see. That in itself is not a sin-"

"Oh, the videos were of me in the shower."

Okay... "I see. Do you want to explain more about this sin, and we shall work together on how we can prevent these sins occuring?"

"Oh! Yes I can tell you more. So, like, I set my camera up at the end of the shower. So, obviously, I am completely naked. Then, whilst the water is pouring over me, I rub soap into all of my skin, getting it slippery and wet. It looks really good on camera, like really shiny and smooth and-"

"You do not need to go into-" It was too late, she wasn't listening.

"And then, I rub my hands all over my skin, so I'm soaked through entirely. I get my boobs really soapy, I massage them with the shower gel, rubbing them up and down, so they bounce a little, because people *love* that, then over my stomach...back up to my boobs..."

Samuel realized he was focussing entirely on what she was saying, his mind conjuring images of the buxom woman, the delicious image of her soft features, the shapely thighs. How he wanted to be in that shower with her, grabbing her ass, her stomach...burying his face in those ample breasts...

"I then wash the top of my thighs and hips, my fingers quickly dipping into my pussy, just to tease, you know? I then sort of turn around a bit, so they can see my ass when I wash myself some more. And then - it, like, gets to the good part. So as I'm washing my ass cheeks, I sort of pull my ass about, make it jiggle, you know? So then they can get a sneaky peak of my asshole and pussy? But like it's totally just a taster. Once I'm good and soapy, I spread a bit more you know, fully for my watchers-"

His mind continued to drift. His breath was shaky as he imagined himself plowing into her bountiful bottom... would she scream for him? Would she make him scream? No. *No.* He tried to banish the thoughts, the intoxicating mental images but it was too late. He felt that the blood had already rushed away southward.

No. No. *God, please no.* He could see the erection through his clothes. It was alert and attentive, twitching to the description of the blonde's sinful words. The devil was tempting him and he was weak to it - he was letting him in. He wrestled the thoughts,

*God, please, please help me. I am just a man, I need your love and guidance to get me through...*

"So then like, I lean over and jiggle my boobs and..." He needed to shut her out. Shut her words out before he was driven insane by lust.

*But I say, walk by the Spirit, and you will not gratify the desires of the flesh. God please.* He continued to think of scripture, trying to fight the intrusive desire to watch those breasts jiggle, to feel them in his mouth-

*Beloved, I urge you as sojourners and exiles to abstain from the passions of the flesh, which wage war against your soul.*

He wanted to feel her soft, hot flesh rub against his own skin, to himself for the first time buried inside her...

*Now the works of the flesh are evident: sexual immorality, impurity, sensuality, idolatry, sorcery, enmity, strife, jealousy, fits of anger, rivalries, dissensions, divisions, envy, drunkenness, orgies, and things like these. I warn you, as I warned you before, that those who do such things will not inherit the kingdom of God.*

He looked down at his hands. He had grasped them so tightly that the fingers were red and sore with friction marks on his own skin. He was shaking, his body desperately seeking to fulfill the urges the darkest parts of his mind were encouraging.

No. He would be strong. With every fiber of his being, and every ounce of mental strength he continued to seek guidance in the bible,

*For the desires of the flesh are against the Spirit, and the desires of the Spirit are against the flesh, for these are opposed to each other, to keep you from doing the things you want to do.*

Yes. He would not be against the Spirit. He would not do these things he wanted so desperately to do.

*No temptation has overtaken you that is not common to man. God is faithful, and he will not let you be tempted beyond your ability, but with the temptation he will also provide a way of escape, that you may be able to endure.*

Yes. God would not let him endure anything he could not handle. This was all a test. A test of his fortitude and faith. He would not fail. It had been two weeks. He would of course be tested by God - everyone knew this. He *knew* this. Dolly was sent by the devil, he would defeat this temptress of evil, he would -

"So like, are you still there?"

"A-Apologies." He had stopped listening long ago, he was unsure of what else had been said. But he knew he needed to help this woman, to save her from the devil.

"It's okay! Just wanted to check that you were, like, alive and stuff, you know?"

"Yes. Thank you. So, my child. You mentioned, in great detail, that you have been committing sins of the flesh and tempting other people. You repented last week but you have sinned again, why do you think that is?"

"Well, I thought about what you said, you know? Like God forgives when I repent, right?"

"That is right."

"So like, every week is a fresh start. And every Sunday, it gets like, wiped clean, I'm forgiven. So I need to do it all over again, so God can forgive me."

"That...that is not how it works. You need to repent. That means that you are truly sorry for everything that you did. That you will not do it again."

"But didn't God like, make us in his image?"

"He did."

"And then like, shouldn't I put that image out there, so like, everyone can see it? Cos like, God made me, and therefore, spreading me, is like, spreading God...and that's like...the point, isn't it?"

Samuel sat for a moment in complete bemusement. Surely she knew that was not how it worked? That presenting herself...her *complete* self, to the world was not what God had intended. That was mortal sin...that was... he could not fathom the words.

"No...No. I think, perhaps, confessional is not the right time to discuss all of this. Perhaps, we need to meet up, and talk more about God, and what he wants and expects from his followers and..."

"Like a date?"

"No...No. Like a class. Where I answer all of your *questions* and we work towards a holier path."

"Oh!" He could hear the excitement in her voice, "Like, is Wednesday good? I have like a kink party tomorrow, and a guy off tinder Tuesday and some content Tuesday night and-"

"Wednesday is fine." He cut her off. "I think, perhaps, we have a lot of work to do."

# III.

Samuel found himself almost nervous as he watched the clock waiting for Dolly to arrive. It was 5pm on Wednesday and she was due any minute. He kept glancing at the clock on the wall, then to the doorway. He held a bible firmly in his hands, stroking the spine gently trying to calm his racing mind. It had taken all of his power to control himself on Sunday. He was aware that God was testing him and he needed to prove that he deserved his position in this church. If he could help Dolly - there would be nothing he couldn't do.

As always he could hear her before she came into view. Each time he heard the familiar rhythmic clack on the cobbles outside, his heart would skip a beat and he felt a weight pull down in his stomach. He both dreaded and loved that sensation. It was exciting and new - it reminded him of the first time he'd stepped inside a grand Cathedral and witnessed the majesty and beauty that belief could create. He shook the thought free. Women - and flesh especially - was not comparable to the art created in the name of God. And yet...

"Priest Samuel!" She greeted him with a smile. Her low cut blouse revealed the sinful mounds of flesh beneath. "You are gonna be so proud of me!"

"Oh?"

"I have panties on today! And...even a bra! How good

is that!?" She smiled, so obviously pleased with herself. He swallowed. Baby steps. This wasn't going to be an overnight miracle. This would take time and work, and it was clear that she was moldable and impressionable - with the right guidance she could be one of the most devout followers. An honest, modest and good woman. She had strayed - that was all. Many people did - the devil was clever in his tricks but, and Samuel had resided himself to the idea, this woman would be saved.

"That is very commendable. Good girl." He found himself saying the words with very little thought, but the blonde stopped in her tracks behind him and gave a wild smile. Samuel was unsure what he had done but brushed it off, she deserved praise for when she tried hard - positive reinforcement would help get her back on track.

"Thank you, Priest Samuel." A shiver ran up his spine - there was something different when she said that. He wasn't sure what it was, perhaps the recognition that he was trying to help? It felt exciting. They would make headway. It was settled.

"So, Dolly. Take a seat for me." He gestured to the chair in his office,

"Yes, Priest Samuel." She looked almost demure, her green eyes staring up at him as she took a seat.

"I want you to tell me what you think it means to be a Christian, and to serve Christ and God." She thought for a moment, twirling her hair around a finger. Her nails were long and pink and her long hair wound and fell, wound and fell - it was strangely mesmerizing.

"Well, I think it's important to like, serve people. I remember that was in the bible. To be submissive." He was impressed,

"Yes, good girl that's right! Can you tell me about a

time you were submissive or served other people before yourself?" She blushed again, biting her lip and the shivers came back.

"Oh yes! I am *very* submissive. I'll happily let people do whatever they want to me. I like to be tied up or spat on. I don't mind a little bit of water sports sometimes, you know? Like, I didn't think it would be my thing, and then I reminded myself about serving others, and it was what the guy wanted, so I thought, what the hell- sorry, the heck, and I did it. And actually, it was super fun. Like for someone to have that much control over you and to use you and for you to do everything they say-"

"Dolly, no...no." How had she misunderstood him so entirely? "That isn't what I meant." He swallowed, the mental pictures of the blonde tied up slowly fading into his mind's eye. He could see the ropes around her soft flesh and her spread thighs and her- No. No he was stronger than this.

"Oh, sorry Priest Samuel." She looked downcast. "I thought that's what you meant. I've always been told I'm very submissive."

"No, the things you are describing are pleasures of the flesh. It's lust. Do you know what lust is?" She nodded. "Good. Lust is a mortal sin, Dolly. We need to repress our desire for it. We need to forgo the earthly pleasures so that we can be rewarded in God's Kingdom." She nodded but he could tell she wasn't fully understanding. "Dolly, do you understand what I mean when I say you need to repress your desire?" She chewed her lip for a moment, her tongue flicking out as she pondered. Samuel found his eyes drifting towards it, as it ran slowly over her lip, her teeth slowly pulling the flesh in...it was hardly anything but...

"I think so. Like chastity?"

"Yes! Amazing, good girl. Exactly like chastity." She beamed to herself, blushing.

"So like, abstaining from sex and stuff, so that it's better later."

"Exactly like that." She beamed again, "Well done Dolly, I think we're reaching an understanding."

"So, should I get, like, a chastity belt?"

"I'm sorry, I don't follow?" He paused. What was a chastity belt? He'd never heard of such a contraption. It sounded like something one of the *other* branches of christianity might use, but he'd never seen or heard of one.

"You know, like a leather set of panties that someone has the key for so that you can't, you know, touch yourself, or have sex or stuff without their permission." She blushed. Samuel felt himself recoil. How interesting. A device to help people refrain from sin - why wasn't this used more often, it could surely save so many souls?
He nodded, "Usually, I would advise to build up the mental fortitude and to learn to resist the urges. But, if you think this will help you Dolly, I think that would be a fantastic idea."

"And I can give you the key?" He felt the blood rise to his cheeks. He was not expecting that. Of course it made sense, and who else could she trust to help her manage her unholy desires. He could think of no reason not to support her. He felt the pressure in his stomach rush southward, his member flickering to life. Why did the thought of holding her chastity bring him such pleasure? This was godly - this was a selfless act to help this woman move towards God but he could feel it infecting his mind, the power he would have over her.
No. He would only use it for good. He would only use it to help her fight her primal urges and become closer to the

Lord.

"Yes, Dolly. If you feel it is best, I will hold the key."

"Thank you Priest Samuel. I'll sort it out and bring it as soon as I can."

"Good. I think that is best." His eyes casted over her. Her soft features reminded him of Bordone's Venus, the elegant rounded curves and flesh - it was art. No. He needed to stop this foolishness. He was being tempted by her flesh. He needed to discuss this with her before anything further occurred and led him astray.

"Dolly, we need to talk about your...outfits."

She looked down at her clothes, "Is there something wrong with them, Priest Samuel? I thought they made me look really hot!" She wasn't wrong...

"See, I think that might be where the problem lies, Dolly. God teaches us that we need to be modest. This means that we should cover up parts of ourselves that are *inappropriate.* So, in church, it's advised to cover your shoulders, very devout people might cover their hair. But you should definitely cover your, erm, chest." She stared at him blankly. "Your erm, bosom." Her eyes widened.

"Oh! Like, so people can't see stuff?"

"Yes. Exactly that." He swallowed, pushing on, "When...people dress in certain ways, it can distract from what they should be doing. Does that make sense?"

"Yes! That's part of the fun. I mean that, and I feel really good about it, like, I know it looks good, if that makes sense."

"Yes, and that is very good that you feel good- but, consider that people may then have impure thoughts about you - especially at church when they should be praying - or worshiping God. You might find that if you cover yourself up, especially in church, that people might give you more...

respect."

"But if they can't, like, focus, that's their fault. Like God knows what I look like, so why do I need to hide it?" This was perhaps more challenging than he had anticipated and he got the impression that she would have an answer for everything.

"Dolly. I would like it if you dressed more modestly at church."

"Yes, Priest Samuel." He watched her huge green eyes widen before she looked down.

"Do we have an understanding?"

"Yes, Priest Samuel."

"Good girl. Now, I will see you on Sunday. Bring your key like we agreed. I expect to see you dressed appropriately - like a good christian woman. I will meet with you again next Wednesday for counseling around your *desires*. Okay?"

She bit her lip again and he felt his erection twitch to life again when she spoke. "Yes, Priest Samuel." He felt his heartbeat quicken. He needed her to leave before the devil took over his thoughts.

"You may leave." She nodded politely, kept her eyes downcast, and toddled out of the door. He stole a glance at her ass sway as she did so, the perfect round peach bouncing with each step. He immediately forced himself to look away - he would not succumb to this.

# IV.

Samuel found himself counting down the days until Sunday. He'd always enjoyed the holy day, but, despite his best efforts, he was anticipating seeing Dolly again. He found himself obsessively wondering what she would be wearing. Would she be covered up? Would she have purchased the device she mentioned and would she really give him the key? It was hard to deny that he found himself flustered and he was unsure why. He'd prayed upon the temptation and sinful thoughts she gave him, but as of yet, God had not answered and nor had he made this challenge easier.

He greeted each person as they filtered in, as he had done the weeks before. He smiled inwardly as he heard the familiar clack on the cobbles. What he didn't expect was the rousing of his member, twitching shamefully to life at the sound of her footsteps. He took a quick glance down - it was not yet visible. He shuffled slightly to ensure it remained hidden. His eyes then caught sight of the blonde. She was wearing her usual high heels, but rather than the tight miniskirts or dresses, she was wearing an *almost* respectable dress. It flowed around her knees and covered her shoulders as well as most of her ample chest. The only *problem* with it, was that in the bright sunlight, it was almost see-through, allowing his eyes to gaze at her shapely thighs which kissed each other with every step. He could see the faint outline of her lace panties. His heart rate quickened and his inner conscience told him to look away - but he couldn't. With the sunlight behind her, shadows casting onto the churchyard, she looked angelic, a vision of heaven walking towards him. Perhaps this was the sign he had prayed upon- perhaps Dolly was not sent by the devil?

He greeted her politely,

"Priest Samuel!" She gave a little twirl, "What do you think?" She beamed at him, the pink lipstick perfectly framing her lips, her green eyes wide and hopeful,

"This is much better Dolly, this is a great improvement. Well done."

She skipped a little, "Oh! I have the-"

"Yes. Yes." He cleared his throat, cutting her off before she spoke, "You may give it to me after communion today." She nodded happily and bounced towards her seat.

No matter how hard he tried, he could not keep his eyes off the blonde on the third row. She looked at him so intently that she appeared to be soaking in every word he spoke. He tried to look around at some of the more bored or uninterested faces - the masses of obliging and good people before him, but none of them held his attention like she did. He could see her long nails wrapped around her bible, the curve of her face moving when she sang.

For the first time, Priest Samuel was coming to the realization that he was obsessed with Dolly.

Like King Herod hunting down children his mind was fully occupied with thoughts of Dolly and how he could see her more, and fulfill his darkest desires of possessing her entirely. He wanted her and he hated this conclusion. He needed to be good, to be holy and rip these thoughts from his brain. As he stood preaching ahead of inviting the congregation to the confessional, he found that the most repressed and darkest parts of his mind were surfacing.

How could someone who looked like her be sent by the devil? He had seen her walk in this morning - surely it was a sign that Dolly was entirely what God had intended for him.

The sermon finished and Samuel advised the mass that following confession, there would be a communion for those who had confessed their sins and were ready to accept the body and blood of Christ.

He took his seat as usual and his heart leaped when he heard the familiar voice filter through. He risked a sideways glance to see the unmistakable profile,

"Bless me father for I have sinned, it has been one week since my last confessional." The soft tones washed over him. Regardless of what she said, he was quietly thrilled to hear her voice.

"Tell me of your sins."

"So, I, like, bought the chastity belt but, like, I needed to get a few things out of my system before I was giving it all up, you know? But, you'll be so pleased, I didn't, like, do anything with *penises*..." She almost whispered the word before carrying on. "So I like, met up with some girlfriends - some of whom are married, but like, I checked everything and God loves lesbians. Like there is literally nothing about girl on girl being a sin, so I figured that it's totally okay. And we went to a party and decided we'd just have a lot of fun in the main room? Obviously, some of the husbands were there, so we invited them to watch, which I think is really kind of good, so they knew that their wives weren't cheating and stuff, you know?
Anyway, I ended up with this woman, fully sitting on my face, like my tongue was buried inside her, I couldn't see

what was going on, and I could hardly breathe. I was being suffocated, but also, I really enjoyed it, you know?"

Samuel looked down and saw his erection flickering to life. With every word Dolly spoke it was becoming harder and harder, the blood flushing into the engorged member. She was the first person in the booth - he would need a level head to discuss the other sins. He looked up to the heavens, fidgeting uneasily in his seat...dear God...was this what he intended?

He had been left with no choice.

He pulled up his cassock, trying to make no sound with his shuffling, and freed his straining member. He struggled to stand in the small box, but he was desperate, and kept glancing over his shoulder to ensure the blonde had not noticed his movement. She was deeply focussed on her story and so, he carefully took his seat again, holding his length firmly in his palm. He stroked the tip a few times with his thumb, building the confidence to do the unthinkable. It was necessary, he reminded himself. He felt the member stiffen to completion, hardened wood in his fingers, his cool hand against the burning hot skin. Then, as he continued to listen to the confession, he began to stroke the shaft. It had been so long. He was tender and twitching. His hand slowly moved up and down, up and down, appeasing the lust that had built within him. He bit his lip, suppressing any sound as he continued to listen to Dolly's words,

"And then she put her fingers, like, fully inside me, like really scissoring and stretching you know, so that Olive could get her tongue in. So between them, I was being fingered and licked out and suffocated and strangled and honestly, like, it was insane. I just had four women all over me and I felt so turned on and wet. Like, someone was playing with my tits too, squeezing them and sucking my nipples and-"

He continued to stroke himself, his hand rubbing up and down, the head becoming more swollen and strained with every brush. He could feel mind focusing on her words, the mental images of Dolly underneath other women, her body being touched and licked and shared... He stroked harder and faster, muting the moan that was caught in his throat. This moment would be between him and God. No one would ever know the secret of what he was doing, the necessary evil so that he may help others. The more he listened, the more he found himself growing angry - angry at these women who got to touch her, angry that they, without fear, could run their hands over her skin and taste her upon their lips. How dare they? He ached for her. He needed her. She would be his. And when he got the key, she would be his - he would control this part of her, this insatiable lust and he would have it to himself. Dolly would be his, and no one else would be able to touch her.

He could feel a searing heat rising in his brain, the burning of his desire boiling his now hot blood. His skin was prickling and tingling with electric waves. He bit his lip, the strain of holding himself together was almost too much to bear,

"And anyways, I was pretty sure the other girls were fuc-having intercourse besides me, I could feel them rubbing against my skin when they were touching my tits and stuff. Anyway, obviously I came. But, I think that wasn't so bad. Like it wasn't with a guy or anything, and like I said, I'm pretty sure that's what's counted right, in the bible and stuff? Plus, I didn't even have sex, it was just tongue and hand stuff with other women, and the bible doesn't say anything about that, but like, just in case,

because like, I think it should count, I wanted to confess..."
Samuel shuddered as he exploded, the air escaping his
throat in a gasp, his head banging against the wooden walls
as he threw it back in silent ecstasy. He looked down at the
horror in his hands. What had he done!?

"Is everything okay?" Dolly's voice came from beside
him,

"Um, yes, yes." He looked around wildly, "I just
banged my head. Saw a..erm, spider and tried to move."

"Oh I hate it when that happens."

He breathed a sigh of relief, she seemed to accept his
excuse. He still needed to clean up.

"So, erm- I think-" He began taking his shoe off
quietly, removing his sock. "I think you have taken great
steps forward in controlling your lust. Abstaining from
men is a commendable start. You do need to abstain from
everyone until marriage, ideally, and-"

"Yeah but still!"

"Yes." He coughed, mopping up the mess with the
sock, before turning it inside out and putting it back on.
He frowned to himself, he had never sunk so low. The sock
now felt soggy and sin covered and he was disappointed
in himself for letting his thoughts get the better of him.
"We-we should pray." He recited the forgiveness prayer
with Dolly. He asked afterwards, "Will you be taking
communion?"

"Oooh, yes! That sounds fun!" And with that, the
door closed, and the dulcet tones of Mrs Norrington came
through. He knew that she was going to complain about
her son and his wild, anti-christian games again. He was
correct.

Confession felt like it had lasted forever. Dolly had
usually come last on her previous visits, giving him the

hope of her voice to look forward to - this time, she'd been first and everyone else by comparison was dull and mediocre. How could he think like that? He shook his head. These were God's followers. They committed minor sins - sins that *other* denominations wouldn't even count. He shuffled in his seat, the sock now growing stiff against his ankles. He would confess himself later. He was thankful that only God would know his secret, and moreover, following the signs today, he was almost sure that Dolly was intended for him.

Following confession he took his place at the altar and Mrs Stevenson brought him the bread and wine. He blessed it in front of the congregation and explained the holy symbolism of the items, and that those who accepted them were accepting Christ.

He watched as each person filed forward, taking a sip from the cup and placed the bread in their mouths. He felt better. This was how it was supposed to be. He felt calm, for a moment, everything was right with the world.

Holding his shoulders back, a relaxed, easy expression on his face, he gave a gentle smile as Dolly knelt before him. He offered her the cup and she took a small sip. He then broke the bread but as he went to hand it to her, found her waiting, her mouth open, tongue slightly protruded. Her huge green eyes stared up at him.

She was on her knees. At his feet. Mouth open. Eyes wide. He found himself lost for words, his imagination suddenly running wild with ideas. Ideas of her being there, bound, chaste, waiting for his command. The sinful explosion in the confession booth covering her pretty face, the fluid dripping down her chin and onto her breasts... his heart pounded and it felt like time had stopped.

He needed to do something, she was waiting. Why

was she not holding out her hands? He took the bread and placed it gently in her mouth. She closed mouth around his fingers, sucking gently as she moved the bread aside. He slowly withdrew the digits. Her eyes casting downwards as she did so.

He pulled them away, his gaze never leaving her. He felt himself stirring inside again. What had just happened? It was as if there was no one else in the world at that moment. His fingers were still wet. He watched, mesmerized as she chewed the bread, before completing the sign of the cross. She stood up, placed a small key in his hand, and then without saying a word and walked away.

Samuel stood, dumbfounded. He could still feel the wetness on his fingers, the stiffness in his sock. He had no thoughts left in his mind, he was fully occupied by Dolly. He needed her. In every unholy and unbiblical way, he needed her. He needed to feel that warmth on his fingers, and the sunlight from her voice. He was unable to think of anything or anyone else.

And so it was decided.

God had made it clear that Dolly should be his.

Hosea had always been his favorite book.

# V.

Samuel sat in his office. He stared into the forgiving eyes of Christ, framed on his desk. The guilt welled up in his stomach and he turned the photo to the table. He swallowed. God had surely willed this, there was no other reason for this unholy woman, this jezebel in his church.

He'd worked so hard, for so long. He'd kept himself pure and gracious and walked in the light. But she was so... enticing. She was so full of excitement and wonder and had so little regard for her eternal soul. It was captivating and he did not know why.

He needed her. He could feel the obsession rising like the waters rose before the flood. Soon it would overspill and destroy everything impure.

It was the only way.

He needed her.

He needed to possess her.

To own her.

He needed her to serve him.

To be on her knees with her huge doe eyes staring up at him as she...

There was nothing else for it.

*For what will it profit a man if he gains the whole world and forfeits his soul? Or what will a man give in exchange for his soul?*

He picked up the corded telephone and with trembling fingers dialed the numbers on the scrap of paper he had kept. As the sharp rings of the telephone cut through the pensive silence his eyes fell on the little chastity key. It sat, inconspicuously besides the keys for the church, the keys to the crypts and the relics. He found his fingers gently reaching towards it.

As his fingertips touched the metal, he felt a strange electric buzz ripple through his veins. The lingering cold of the metal leaving a strange ache as his blood turned cold. He found himself yearning for Dolly's touch, for her warmth. He wanted desperately to feel her fingers on his skin, feel her warm tongue upon his flesh...

*Nothing good dwells in me, that is, in my flesh; for the willing is present in me, but the doing of the good is not.*

"Hello?" The soft tone pulled him from his thoughts. He cleared his throat, stammering to respond,

"H-Hello. This is Priest S-"

"Samuel! Hello! It's Dolly!"

"Y-Yes, I know. I called you..."

There was a pause. "Oh yes, you did. Silly me."

"I..." He took a steadying breath, "I wanted to invite you to another...class." He swallowed, his mind racing. "To help with your situation." His thoughts rallied and he could feel his confidence growing. He could hear her smile through the phone.

"That sounds fun! I have some time this evening! It's super hard to film with a chastity belt, so I can take a break."

"Film with the chastity belt on? Isn't the point of..."

"Well, I can't have *sex*. But there are always *other* things." She giggled.

"Dolly, I think it's best you come sooner, rather than later."

"Yes Daddy!"

"It's Father!" But she had already hung up. He sat for a moment in the pensive silence. He looked down at his erection, clearly visible in his black trousers. No more would she elude him.

He would make Dolly his. She would scream out for God...for him...

His mind was racing and he found that he kept glancing out of the office window. Was she on her way now? When would she be here?

What was his plan? Would he lecture her? Or would he take her like a man takes his wife? Over his desk and plough into her again and again and again, each thrust bringing him closer to the nirvana of heaven...No. No. He shook his head.

He needed to do this right. Perhaps if she was his - *officially* - then there would be no sin. Dolly would be saved - he would be saved. They could have children and live a holy, respectable life.

But he had made a vow of chastity.

He had forsworn women and pleasures of the flesh.

He thought back to the confessional. He had been weak. But, God truly did forgive all sins.

He would understand. He had sent Dolly - Samuel was sure of this.

*Among them we too all formerly lived in the lusts of our flesh, indulging the desires of the flesh and of the mind.*

He tried to busy himself with tidying papers, with menial tasks. It was no good. He constantly found himself looking out of the window. He even took a walk to the graveyard, wondering if he'd see her approach, but nothing. He knew he should eat soon, take a cup of tea, but he was too distracted. He was waiting for her, and he was hoping she would arrive soon. The anticipation was building in his stomach, strangling him at the throat. Without her he felt like a lost lamb and Dolly was the shepherd - leading him to where he needed to be.

No.

No.

*He* was the Shepherd. *He* would lead her. Away from sin. He recited this in his mind over and over. He was in control. He knew what he needed to do.

And then he heard the gentle clatter of heels of cobblestones.

He felt his manhood stir in his pants. The blood flowing southwards at the sound of her heels on flagstones.

*But each one is tempted when he is carried away and enticed by his own lust.*

He closed his eyes, counting softly under his breath. He needed desperately to control himself, he needed to be strong to do this. He could do this...he could-

"Father Sam!" He felt the shiver run up his spine. He opened his eyes.

"Dolly." He smiled softly. He stood before him, her dress slightly disheveled, the strap hanging low on her arm, the top of her breast fully exposed and a hint of her areola on display. He was drawn to it and his mouth turned dry.

Her blonde hair cascaded over her shoulders, tousled and messy, but her makeup was perfect. Her lips perfectly plump and her large eyes staring up at him through dark lashes. He felt the quiver of his erection and he pulled himself back into the moment.

"I think you should come inside." He managed and she beamed,

"It's always better to come inside." She giggled as she totted inside her hips swaying as she entered the door to God's house.

# VI.

Dolly sat across from Samuel. It felt like an eternity as she stared into his eyes, waiting.

"So." He smiled nervously, "Dolly."

"Yes Dad-Father."

"I wanted to discuss your behavior and try to help get to the bottom of what is going on and help you manage your sins."

"That makes sense. You're so nice!" She beamed.

"Yes." He cleared his throat. "You mentioned that you are still doing *other* things, despite wearing a chastity belt?" He felt the blush rise to his cheeks. Her lips curved into a knowing smile.

"Oh yes. It's one of the key ways that I make money."
He nodded,

"Go on?"

"So like, I offer a text and phone call service - like, I talk dirty to people for money. They pay me to respond and..."

"Talk...dirty?" He cut her off. "I'm sorry Dolly, I'm not sure what you mean..." His brow furrowed as he frowned, gently licking his lips.

Her lips cracked wider into a grin, "Oh! I can tell you. So like, they might ask what I'm wearing, and I'll tell them I have *nothing* on. I'll tell them that I'm wet or slick and ready for them to slip their hard dicks inside me. I talk about how

I'd scream over and over as I feel their huge dick filling me up, stretching me. Maybe I'd talk about touching my tits and my nipples as they bounce up and down along with me riding them. Sometimes I talk about how much I want them to cum on my face, or on my tits and cover me in their sticky fluid and how I'm a good girl and I'll savor it and rub it all into my skin..."

Samuel let out a little whimper.

"I see." His voice cracked. "And are all these things true?"

"Well, it's a text or phone service, so I'm not *actually* doing them. But it does get me super wet and sometimes I need to play with myself to release all the horniness it builds up. If that makes sense?"

It made perfect sense. Samuel could feel his own desire stretching his trousers. He could feel it threatening to break free. Dolly glanced over at him, writhing with obvious discomfort.

"Do you need some help?" She said sweetly, her voice dripping with sugary tones, "You look uncomfortable." She began rummaging in her little bag, "Like, I've got some pain killers and some stomach tablets and some..."

"No. No. It's quite alright." He shuffled again, desperately trying to hide his shame.

"We could go for like, a little walk or something? Like that always helps me feel better." She began to stand up.

"No!" He snapped, his wild eyes looking around the room. He needed to regain control. Needed to focus again. She sat down quickly. "Sorry." He cleared his throat again. "It will pass. I think it is more important that we focus on you... and your...sins." He swallowed. "I think we are getting off track..." He dug his short nails into his thigh, hoping that the pain would distract him. He could feel his eyes wandering, his mind losing focus as he stared at her soft lips. What he would do to see them…

"Yes." She looked demure. "Father Samuel?"

"Yes, Dolly." His heart and mind were racing,

"I really like it when you tell me what to do." She licked her lips, gently biting them as she did so. "Do you think maybe you could do it *more?*" Her huge eyes looked at him as she drew little circles with her fingers on the edge of the desk. Samuel's mind went completely blank. There was *so much* he wanted to tell her to do, so many things he *yearned* for and *needed.* He gave a little cough as he tried to refocus.

"Yes, Dolly. Let us start with these…phone calls." She nodded. "You said that you…masturbate afterwards?" She smiled happily and nodded, "And have you been able to do that…" He swallowed hard, glancing down at her legs, "With the belt on?" For a moment he could have sworn he saw a blush creep onto her cheeks.

"See, Father, that's the problem. I can't wank with the belt on. So all the horniness has been building up. I feel like I might burst soon. *Everything* is turning me on." He found himself speechless again,

"Everything?" He choked the words out.

"*Everything.*" She whispered. He gulped, his mouth falling slightly open. His mouth was moving before he had a chance to think - had the devil taken control?

"Could…Could you give me some examples?"

Dolly licked her lips, her pink tongue slowly caressing the dark lipstick. "Well, it's turning me on when you tell me what to do…" she knotted her hands together, "And I keep thinking about how you would look in nothing other than your little priest collar or scarf…" Her huge eyes looked up at him, bearing into his damned soul, "And every time I look at my rosary, I've been thinking of places I could put it...and how I could say a little prayer with *every* bead..." Samuel almost choked on his saliva.

"Stop, stop. I've heard enough." He shook his head and the woman before him clamped shut her lips. His erection was pressing firmly against his trousers now, the fabric was at its breaking point and his flesh was begging for release from its confinement.

"Yes, Father." She smiled gently. Samuel could feel his heart pounding. His head was light as if every fluid ounce of blood had rushed southwards. He needed to stop this, or else the devil would take him completely.

"Dolly. I want you to stop doing the phone lines."

"And the texts?"

"And the texts. Dolly, let me make myself perfectly clear." He felt a sudden power build up inside him, as if the almighty were giving him courage. He knew what he had to say and do.

"Dolly, you are to have no further sexual discussions or sexual intimacy with anyone. I do not want you to touch them, and I certainly don't want them to touch *you.* You are not to engage in chat lines, texting or any *online* activities. I want you to be chaste and holy."

He could feel his voice almost trembling. He steadied himself as he took out the chastity belt key, slamming it on the desk as he stood. "You entrusted me with this, and I take this responsibility *very* seriously. It is the case of your immortal soul, and *I will* save you-IT. You will give yourself to no person without my *express* permission. Have I made myself clear?" He looked down at her, her mouth agape. Had he gone too far? It was too late now. "Dolly - Have I made myself clear?" He tried again. In a moment of annoyance he followed her gaze. He realized it was not in fact, at his face, but directly at his crotch. He glanced down, and realized to his horror, that in his assertiveness, he had forgotten to hide his arousal, and there was no mistaking that the curvaceous blonde was now fully aware of it.

*Those who indulge the flesh in its corrupt desires and despise authority. Daring, self-willed, they do not tremble when they revile angelic majesties.*

# VII.

It was too late now. She had seen. Samuel's heart felt as though it might beat out of his chest. He wished it would, and end the embarrassment that had consumed him. He felt his cheeks burn. He kept his face stern, he could not falter now. He needed to maintain this authority, it was *all* he had left. He watched as she dragged her eyes up his body to meet his own. As she did, she stood up from her chair, her gaze locked intently on his own. He could feel his breath shaking, his resolve wavering. He stared into the bright green eyes and in that moment, felt the warm, delicate hand cover his erection. He opened his mouth to protest but found no words, her eyes still locked firmly on his own.

> *I want you to swear, O daughters of Jerusalem,*
> *Do not arouse or awaken my love*
> *Until she pleases*

He glanced down at her lips, they were so soft, so *inviting.* Her hand was already there, gently squeezing. He *needed* this. She was surely sent to him. No other temptress, no other challenge had been so alluring. It was God's will. He was *certain.* How else could she be here? Could she have such control? The devil himself could have no such power over him, he was so sure. He glanced again at her lips.

> *But if they do not have self-control, let them marry; for*

*it is better to marry than to burn with passion.*

That would be the solution. He knew it before and he now knew it with unwavering certainty. And with that, he pulled his hand from the desk, wrapped it around Dolly's waist and pulled her in closely, pushing his lips upon her own.

He had never felt anything like this. It was more beautiful than his mind could have conjured. Her lips were warm and soft. They pressed hard against his own as a small gasp escaped her mouth. As she did so, he felt the wet flesh of her tongue against his lips. He opened his mouth instinctively, feeling his own tongue respond so naturally to hers. His pulse began to quicken and he pulled her closer, closer than he thought possible. He could feel her breasts pushed against his chest, the small of her back arched into his grip. His spare hand automatically found its way to her hair, tangling his fingers into it, pulling her deeper into his first kiss. He felt as her hand squeezed his erection again and he felt a moan escape his mouth for the first time unstifled and unbound. He felt the blonde smile as she did it again, her fingers gently fumbling at his pants to loosen them. He was too caught up and he could not stop this now, not even if he wanted to.

They were in the church offices, perhaps this was the best place, for here, under God's witness, he would lose his self control and he would then make Dolly his, *forever.* They would be bound to each other, and he would tame her into his wife. He knew he could do this, he knew he would...

He moaned again as his manhood was pulled free of his pants, springing free of its constraints. The next moan stifled in his throat as for the first time, he felt her bare hand upon his flesh, her fingers encircling his engorged penis.

Slowly, she began to move her hands up and down, up to the tip and down to the base. He groaned softly into her mouth.

"Father, should I stop?" She whispered. He opened his eyes a fraction to see her pleading eyes, confused and aroused.

"No. You must carry on." His hand made its way to hers, squeezing with encouragement, he needed her to continue, he could feel his member twitch in her hand. This had to continue. "God has decided that this must happen. He has brought us together." She smiled seductively,

"I understand." She began to stroke again, and with the hand in her hair, he pulled her in again for a long, passionate kiss.

He could feel the wetness of her mouth upon his own, the saliva that threatened to drip from their lips. He could feel her stroking, the rhythmic, entrancing motion. *This was happening.* He groaned, moaning further into their kiss.

He could feel his penis throbbing and pulsing, he could feel his rational thoughts leaving his mind, he could feel his lust and passion taking over as his knees grew weak with every stroke of her soft hands.

She continued to work on his manhood, her loose grip tightening as her fingers darted over the head again and down to the base, the pace quickening, all he could see was her, her beautiful eyes, green like the Garden of Eden, fertile and heavenly. Her hair was golden like paintings of halos and her skin was flush like the Madonna in Rapheal's works. He was overcome with passion, with lust like he had never felt. In a swift movement he swiped the items from his desk, knocking them to the floor, pulling the blonde to sit upon it. There, he clambered madly on top of her, all the while clumsily kissing her lips, his mind awash with a blissful focus, like he had never before in his life felt.

This was all so *right*. How could he ever have believed otherwise?

He found his fingers fumbling at her dress, exposing her breasts, tightly encased in pink lace. His chest heaved and mouth ran dry at the sight of them. The paintings of Eve did not bear justice to the body before him and he found himself completely overcome. He felt as though he should go mad. How did anyone bear this? How could they cope?

He felt Dolly's spare hand wander up his chest and to his shirt, slowly unfastening each button. His resolve faltered for a moment, but she pulled him in, kissing him again, her moisture wetting his mouth once more.

He felt the groans escape his mouth and he knew he couldn't take much more, he felt his thoughts escaping him further as the pleasure in his loins built up, taking him over. In a white hot second, he felt himself release upon Dolly's stomach in the middle of their kiss.

She did not stop, she simply pulled back her hand and moved it up his chest, the sticky fluid marking his skin, his heart.

And then it hit him what he had done. The clarity beamed through. But it was too late. She had touched him. He had touched her.

There was no going back now.

He was in *sin*.

*I say to you that everyone who looks at a woman with lust for her has already committed adultery with her in his heart.*

# VIII.

Samuel pulled himself away from Dolly. He took a deep breath.

"I apologize. That should not have happened." He spoke firmly. He knelt down, picking some tissues up from the floor, "Please." He handed them to her. She tilted her head.

"Did I do something wrong?"

"No." He spoke quickly. "It was my fault. I am here to help you become more pious, and instead, I have allowed myself to sin with you. This was not meant to happen."

"Pious?" Dolly cocked an eyebrow,

"Yes. And I fear I have led you astray. I need to atone for what I have done." He turned away from her, fastening his shirt.

"Punish me instead. It's my fault." Samuel shook his head. "I am your Priest, Dolly. I should have been stronger. It will not happen again." A pang of sadness ripped through his chest. How did it come to this? But surely if they had already sinned, if it could be forgiven...if Dolly was from God then it could happen again.

"Punish me, Father." Dolly spoke quietly, "I think I've caused trouble, I've been bad and I should be punished." She bit back a small smile. "I would feel much better if you punished me." Samuel froze for a moment.

"Dolly this is serious..."

"I know." She collected a few items from the floor and handed them over to him. "But *I need* to be punished." The Priest thought for a moment. He looked down at the bible in his hands. It was heavy, and thick.

"Very well. If you feel it will help your eternal soul."

"Oh yes, Da-Father. I believe it will."

"Very well. It will be corporal punishment."

"Of course." Dolly nodded.

*You shall strike him with the rod*
*And rescue his soul from Sheol.*

Samuel took a wide leg stride across his chair and beconned Dolly to lay, face down across his lap. She hiked up her dress baring her soft cheeks to him. Samuel took a sharp inhale of breath.

"Dolly. You will pray between strikes. Do you understand?"

"Yes, Father."

He nodded to himself. "Very well." He pulled back his arm, the heavy book in hand and struck her hard across the buttocks. She called out,

"Oh God!" Samuel swallowed,

"Pray." He hit her again, the skin turning a fiery pink.

"Mmhmm. For-give me." She said breathlessly,

"Continue." He struck again.

"Lord, I..mhmm..."

"Again."

"I s-seek your forgiveness...mhmm" She gasped and cried out between each strike.

"Keep going."

"And-and healing..." She moaned loudly on the next strike,

"Dolly? Are you enjoying this?" Samuel commanded.

The blonde nodded, "Yes, Yes Father."

He shook his head. "This is punishment. I will have to hit you harder."

"Yes...Father." He pulled back his hand again, striking her with the full force of the book, she moaned again.

"Dolly, if you continue this, you will leave me no choice but to be more severe." He struck her again, soft moans falling from her lips. He felt his penis stir in his pants.

*Then the king said to the servants, 'Bind him hand and foot...'*

He nodded to himself, covering Dolly's flesh again.

"You've left me no choice." He shook his head, praying that what he was doing was right. "I command you to take off your clothes. Fold them, and lay them on the table. I need you naked, and modest before God. I will bind you and we will re-baptise you, in hope that you can relinquish yourself of your sin."

Dolly nodded, a small smile upon her face, "Yes. Father." Slowly, she unfastened the remainder of her dress, slipping it over her shoulders and hips until it dropped in a fabric puddle on the floor. She ran her fingers up her arms before turning her back to the priest, unfastening her bra as she did so. She glanced at him over her shoulder, a coy smile on her face. Samuel felt himself blush, forcing himself to keep contact with her eyes.

"And the rest."

"Yes Father." With that she bent over as she slid off her panties, unhooking them with her fingers. She held them on her index for a moment before smirking again at Samuel and dropping them to the floor. She ran her hands over the chastity belt, before turning and walking to the desk. She laid herself across it and spread her legs. "I will need help with this part Daddy. You have the key." She rubbed the lock gently between her fingers.

Samuel stared at her for a moment, completely dumbfounded.

He admitted to himself that he had wanted to see her nude. That there was no *real* reason for a naked baptism... but she had *so willingly* obliged him, surely this showed her keenness to repent? He found his eyes focusing on her thighs. He drank in the full picture before him. She was shapely, womanly and beautiful. She rested herself up on her elbows, placing the key delicately between her lips.

"Dolly." He spoke in a warning tone, "I will not have this foolishness from you." She said nothing but continued to stare up at him. He placed two fingers under her chin, grabbing the top with his thumb. He started into her mischievous eyes and felt himself beginning to drown again. Every inch of his being was calling to him to kiss her again, to take the key with his own lips, unfasten her and give himself to her completely.

It would be too much.

He could not.

He would not.

Could he?

*And the tongue is a fire, the very world of iniquity; the tongue is set among our members as that which defiles the entire body, and sets on fire the course of our life, and is set on fire by hell.*

Before his conscience could stop him, he felt his lips close to hers, pressing themselves against the metal of the key as he took it in his own mouth. He watched as she closed her eyes as he pulled away. He kept his fingers on her chin.

"We will have no more of this."

"Yes, Father." She nodded.

He steadied his hands as he fumbled the lock, releasing the garment. She slid it off. For a moment he took it in. He put the key in his pocket.

"You need to understand. Just because the belt is off, does not mean the rules have changed. Right now, you are as you were when you were brought to earth. Immaculate." He swallowed, trying to create moisture in his mouth again, "No one else will see you like this again, lest they be your husband. Am I clear?"

"Yes Father."

"I still hold the key, and even though the belt is not on, it does not mean the rules have changed. Do you understand?"

"Yes Father."

"Good girl." He paused for a moment, thinking, "Dolly. Tell me the rules."

She sat up on the desk, her legs still wide with all of her womanhood on display. "I will not show anyone my body, except for my husband."

"Good girl."

"I will not take part in any sex acts with myself, or anyone else..." She paused looking for words,

"Without my express permission." Samuel finished.

"Yes, Father."

"And?"

"And?" She raised an eyebrow in perfect innocence. She looked down and gently placed a finger between her legs. She put it to her mouth and sucked it gently, "I'm sorry Father," she dipped her fingers there again, "But I appear to be wet…"

*No temptation has overtaken you but such as is common to man; and God is faithful, who will not allow you to be tempted beyond what you are able, but with the temptation will provide the way of escape also, so that you will be able to endure it.*

"Dolly. Stand up." Samuel commanded. He glanced at the wooden desk, noticing a small wet patch where she had been sitting.

"Do you want to check?" She held her fingers out to him. She smiled sweetly.

"I believe you. Go. Clean yourself up. Then return and fold your clothes." She nodded demurely and walked away to the little bathroom in the office.

As soon as she left Samuel felt a surge of emotion encapsulate him and he threw his fist into the wall. He was erect again and all he could do was think about plunging his cock into the slut.

PENIS.

Penis.

Think about inserting his *penis* into the *woman.* He opened his eyes and looked at the cracked plaster. Blood spattered his knuckles. This woman was driving him to sin. His chest heaved with uncontrolled breathlessness.

He would have her.

Screw everything else. He was already ruined.

He grabbed his stole and marched towards the bathroom.

Dolly would be his. In every way imaginable.

# IX.

Dolly was standing at the sink when Samuel entered behind her. She glanced up in the mirror and saw him walk towards her. As she was about to turn around Samuel placed the holy stole around her shoulders, using the fabric to pull her against him. He inhaled her scent, it was intoxicating and he could feel his heart racing already. Holding the ends of the stole in one hand, he swept her hair from her shoulders with the other, burying his lips in her neck.

He kissed her greedily, licking and kissing anything and everything his lips could touch. Dolly arched her back against him, her butt pushing into him, into his erection. He let his hand fall from her hair, down, over her large breasts, her stomach and hips and down to her legs.

His blood raced through his veins, dizzy with excitement he closed his eyes, letting his hand continue to wander.

He could feel the soft skin under his fingertips, the supple flesh, tender and warm. He could smell her sweet perfume and the hint of soap. It was everything he hoped it would be. He continued to let his hand explore her. It was the first time he had explored another person, and now, he understood. He understood why the Greeks burned Troy to retrieve Helen, he understood how Cleopatra seduced Marc Anthony and Ceasar...it all felt *so clear.*

As he stroked her thighs and bottom he knew why celibacy

was encouraged. How could any man strive for anything better than this? How could he live a holy life in hope of a paradise, when it could be found on earth in a woman's bosom?

For this, he would renounce everything. He would live in sin to be able to do this again and again and again.

His eyes still closed, his fingers maneuvered to her inner thigh. Taking a long, steadying breath, he bit his lips as he slid his fingers over her womanhood. His fingertips touched the delicate line of hair trailing up her pubic bone. He followed the trail downwards, parting her labia as he did so. She arched against him more, a soft gasp escaping her mouth. He continued to feel his way around her, his hand moving backwards to her wet opening.

It was slippier and further back than he had expected, but he coated his fingers in her moisture, rubbing them back and forth over her.

"Mmhmm, F-father." She gasped, "Please don't stop." Her hand encapsulated his, her slender warm fingers moving his upwards to her clitoris. She moaned louder as his guided hand slid over her again and again. He half opened his eyes, seeing her head loll back onto his shoulders, he pulled the stole up to her neck, leaving it to drape over her shoulders so that he could massage her breast. His hand caressed her, puckering the nipple between his thumb and finger, twisting and playing, enjoying the noises that the blonde made.

He could feel himself going wild, his obsession growing, the need to feel her, to touch her, to own her increasing. With one hand on her breasts and one hand on her clit, his face buried hungrily in her neck, he began to feel more than he had ever felt in his life. His mind was racing and he thought he might explode. His mind was battling between a blissful emptiness and a rush of every emotion and thought he'd ever had. She arched again, and this time, he pushed back against her.

"Dolly-" He muttered between wet kisses,

"F-Father..." He pushed against her again, his clothed groin pushing into her bare butt. Electricity twinged through him as he did so, and yearning for the sensation again, he pushed again and again, grinding into her, his fingers flickering between her legs and upon her nipples. He felt himself unable to suppress moans, unable to contain himself any longer. He dropped his hands, turning her around quickly and pulling her against him.

Screw the Church.

Screw God.

He needed to *screw* Dolly.

A voice in the back of his mind called out to him, beckoned him back to the path of righteousness, but he had gone too far. It was too late - he had no chastity and this woman would drive him to sin as long as she was there.

He couldn't let anyone else be tempted by her.

He would not allow it.

She was his.

"Dolly..." He gasped between breaths, "Who do you belong to?"

"You."

"Who do you belong to?"

"I belong to you." She gasped.

"Who do you belong to?"

"Fa-father Samuel." She moaned, his hands back between her legs. "I belong-to to you Father."

"Yes. Good Girl." He continued to massage between her legs, his tongue finding her sinful mouth. He needed more though. It wasn't enough. His tongue left her mouth, dragging itself down her chin and neck. Down through her sternum and navel and past the little trail of hair.

He fell to his knees between her legs, looking up at her.

He could worship her.

*His goddess.*

He gasped, beholding her again.

Then, with the hunger of a thousand people he gripped her ass in both hands, his short nails digging into the flesh as he pushed his face into her legs, dragging his tongue up her legs.

The taste was divine. He dragged his tongue further up, further towards her womanhood.

He needed *more*.

He felt the first inkling of moisture against his tongue. Hungrily he chased the trail up towards her opening.

He groaned in ecstasy as he plunged his face into her vagina, his wet lips and tongue lapping up as much as he could. He squeezed her ass, thrusting her hips towards him as he sucked and licked and devoured her as much as he could.

*You must not eat from the tree of the knowledge of good and evil, for when you eat from it you will certainly die.*

He moaned into her opening, into her flesh. His mind a white hot mess as she buried her hands in his hair.

"More..." She moaned, "I need more. F-fuck me. Please..." He pulled back, her juices still upon his face. He clambered to his feet, pushing his hot, sticking mouth against her own.

"No."

He knew there would be a line. He had tasted the fruit

and there was no going back - he'd never be pope, but...he would not lie with her.

"Please-" She begged, he touched her bottom lip, wiping the wetness from her chin.

"No." He straightened up. "I cannot lie with you, unless we are married."

"F-Father." Dolly begged, putting his hand back on her clitoris, "I'm so wet. Please...please I need...I need *more.*"

And then, Samuel said the thing he subconsciously knew he would say right from the moment he saw her.

"Dolly. Marry me."

# X.

Dolly stared at Samuel. She cocked an eyebrow and gave a half smile,

"Oh Daddy, you're so silly." She pulled him closer, his face meeting her own, "We can't get married yet! We've not even had sex!" She giggled, her hand wandering southwards to his growing arousal. She squeezed roughly through his pants, massaging him heavily, stirring him back to life,

"Dolly, please, I don't want to live in sin." He held her shoulders firmly, looking deep into her green eyes, imploring her, "I cannot stop thinking about you, you've bewitched me. Please - marry me." She shook her head again, her blonde hair cascading over her shoulders.

"Like, one thing I know is that sexual compatibility is super important. Don't you do, like, counseling and stuff for that?" Her face looked serious for a moment, "We need to like 'do it' first. That's not bad is it?"

"Dolly. You're meant to wait until marriage before having carnal relations."

"But then, how would you know you're like, good together? I think we should try first. And then like, if you don't like it, you can repent and stuff, and no harm done, right?"

No harm done. No harm done? Samuel stepped back shaking his head. The woman was Rasputin incarnate. He looked at her desperately, he wanted her with every fiber of his being, every inch and hair and cell longed for her, longed to keep touching her, longed to be on her, *inside her.*

He pleaded again, "Please, *please.* I cannot live in sin. I am a man of God, I promised myself to him...Dolly, *please let me make this right."*

*But if they cannot exercise self-control, they should marry. For it is better to marry than to burn with passion.*

"I like it," She smiled seductively, "When you beg." She licked her lips slowly, her eyes bright, "Ooh, I know what we can do!" She smiled, "I remember in school, there was a loophole that a lot of people did. So they're like, still virgins and stuff." Samuel thought for a moment. There was no loophole, that's not how this worked, unless she meant... his eyes widened. She surely didn't mean?

"I-I-" He stammered,

"Anal!" She said with glee. The Priest's face didn't budge an inch. He felt the shock rippling through him,

"Dolly...that...that isn't a loophole."

"It definitely is." She beamed widely, "Everyone says so. It's like a known thing. Didn't you go to Catholic school?" Her innocent eyes were bright with happiness. Samuel had indeed gone to catholic school, and he had, of course, heard of the 'loophole'. But he was also aware that God didn't like loopholes, and the clergy most definitely didn't think it was a 'loophole' - it just wasn't how things worked.

"I can't." He took a step away from her. "I can't do that to you. I can't do that to myself." He looked downcast, his heart heavy in his chest. The blonde stepped forward again, pressing her chest, leaning forward, whispering in his ear, giggling,

"Okay," her hot breath danced over his skin, "I have another idea! We have sex tonight. We do everything, and then, tomorrow, I disappear. I won't come back or anything, I'll be all mysterious and be gone when you wake up or something. Like a one night stand. And then you can repent and spank yourself or whatever it is you do." She pulled away slowly, her flesh glancing past his own.

He felt the hairs stand up on end as she did so, his mind racing. The woman was *wicked*.

Repent tomorrow.

Sin today.

Never be tempted by her again.

*No temptation has overtaken you that is not common to man. God is faithful, and he will not let you be tempted beyond your ability, but with the temptation he will also provide the way of escape, that you may be able to endure it.*

Maybe this was it. This was his way out. God knew he couldn't be rid of her any other way. That she would forever dance across his mind, that he'd forever hear her heels on cobblestones and see her breasts increased under her sheer shirt in his dreams.

And now he'd *tasted* her. His appetite had been peaked and surely it would never be satiated without the main course. He wanted to feel her dripping onto his tongue, feel her enveloped around him, tight and throbbing. Writhing and moaning, sweating and grinding…

No. This is how it starts. He'd never have enough of her, he knew he'd never be free. He'd long for her, every time he saw her, he would need her again.

*But I say to you that everyone who looks at a woman with lustful intent has already committed adultery with her in his heart.*

But he'd already done this...hadn't he? He had already looked at her with lustful intent. He'd already committed this sin. *Lust.* He closed his eyes, gently breathing in the scent of her. The worn-in perfume, the slight sweat from before. He could smell the dustiness of his office. If she left forever, he'd have no choice. He would sin and sin and sin again if she stayed. He would spiral until he reached the burning gates of hell and nothing would stop him. Could he trust her though? Would it truly be over? One, huge sin, followed by a flogging repent and then be refreshed and clean from her?

He could feel his fingers trembling as he reached out, cupping her jaw under her chin.

"Dolly- I..."

She placed a finger over his lips, and smiled widely. "I promise I'll go."

He swallowed. Was this it then? Was this really his way out?

He had to try, or else be forever tormented by her dancing across his mind. He did not have the strength to escape her, but perhaps she had the strength to walk away and that was all he needed.

"How can I trust you?"

She shrugged, "I've had a one night stand before, Daddy." She bit her lip, her hands reaching up to his soft hair as she ran her fingers through it, "I'm like, literally a pro."

He felt himself gulp involuntarily, his mind racing with every option and possibility.

He wanted this.

He *needed* this.

He nodded slowly and the blonde squealed excitedly.

"We're going to have so much fun! I promise it'll be worth it!" And within a heartbeat she pressed her lips against his, her soft, warm skin against his own.

He felt his mouth open, ready to let her in, ready to accept his fate. She wrapped her arms around him, pulling him closer. He could feel her breath escaping the kiss, her heat enveloping him as he pulled her against him. Samuel didn't think it possible for their bodies to be any closer, he felt almost crushed by closeness, but it felt beautiful, it felt right.

It felt like the one thing he'd been missing his entire life. He ran his fingers over her nude body, careful to feel every inch of her skin, every mound and crevasse. He let his palms feel the curve of her hips, the swell of her ass and his mind flooded with an inescapable pleasure, a level of serene he'd only felt a few times before.

*How beautiful and pleasant you are, O loved one, with all your delights! Your stature is like a palm tree, and your breasts are like its clusters.*

He dragged his fingers to her breasts, kneading them in his palm, teasing the nipple between his fingers. He moaned softly into her mouth as he did so, savoring every touch, every swipe.

*I say I will climb the palm tree and lay hold of its fruit. Oh may your breasts be like clusters of the vine, and the scent of your breath like apples, and your mouth like the best wine. It goes down smoothly for my beloved, gliding over lips and teeth. I am my beloved's...*

He continued exploring her body as he felt her fingers creep under his shirt, her nails gently scratching down his back as she deepened their kiss. Goosebumps arose on his skin, his spine tingling.

"Take it off." He commanded between kisses. His mind was barely functional, barely working and able to fathom thoughts, but Dolly was still his to command, he recalled that much. He needed to remain in control - needed to control the experience.

*Satan may not tempt you because of your lack of self-control.*

He felt Dolly smile against his lips,

"Yes, *Father.*" She whispered, her nails dragging over his back, around his ribs and then down to his navel before pulling outside the shirt. She pulled away from the kiss, her doe eyes watching him as she slowly unfastened each button, her gaze never leaving his as she expertly opened the shirt.

She ran her palms up and over his chest and to his shoulders, before pushing the fabric off his skin. Her hands ran over his arms before a sharp tug to free his wrists.

Samuel silently prayed that he would keep a straight face, that he would last through the experience.

*Pray.* He snorted inwardly. He wished that he could hide this sin from God, but it was too late. He had been tempted and the only way out was to repent. But, he'd come this far - may as well make it worth it.

And then never again.

*Never.*

He let his mind wander, running through language and words he'd never considered using - words that weren't chaste or proper, but they felt *right.* He was pulled from his daze by the gentle voice,

"Now what?"

He raised an eyebrow...now what? He looked at The

Venus before him, his eyes casting over his own body. "What do you think?" The words came easily, but he was unsure what to do. He hoped beyond reason that he could hide his inexperience, his insecurities.

He watched through dark eyes as the blonde ran her fingers over his chest, stroking the contours gently before letting her nails trail southwards to the rim of his pants. She stroked a finger along the waistband, teasing her finger beneath. Samuel tried to steady his heart rate. He closed his eyes and she flicked the button and pulled the trousers apart, opening the zip. She pushed her hands down his back and over his ass, cupping the cheeks before hooking her fingers over the hems, pulling the clothing off slowly. He felt the cold air caress his skin as the fabric fell to the floor. He stepped out of the clothes and towards Dolly, for the first time since his birth, nude before someone else. He could feel the heat radiating off her skin as his chest touched her breasts. He felt them press against him, his skin prickling again under their touch as he wrapped his arms around her, pulling her closer again for a deep kiss.

He felt his hands tangle in her hair, increasing the pressure between their lips, the force almost enough to bruise.

He felt her gasp as his fist gripped her hair, his erection growing and pressing against the softness of her legs. He could feel his blood racing, his cheeks burning as he continued to stroke his hands over her.

This was it then.

# XI.

*Do not deprive one another, except perhaps by agreement for a limited time, that you may devote yourselves to prayer; but then come together again.*

He felt Dolly pull away from the kiss, his hands still entangled in her hair as she kissed down his neck, his chest and thighs before settling in front of his manhood. Her huge green eyes looked up at him as her tongue flicked along the tip of his erection. He closed his eyes, squeezing her hair tightly as her hot tongue danced around the head of his penis before dragging down to the base, swirling around his warm skin. He let out a low groan as she repeated the movements, becoming slightly faster with each cycle, her feather-soft lips catching his shaft every now and then. He could feel his heart pounding like never before, his blood rushing southward as all rational thinking escaped him. There was nothing but him and Dolly, the world around them ceased to exist. He felt the heat of her mouth envelop him entirely. He felt the wetness and fire of her tongue, her lips closing around him as she moved from base to tip over and over.

Moans escaped his lips as her hands grasped at his strong thighs, her fingers moving to his ass, which she squeezed as if holding on for dear life as she moved her head faster and faster.

Samuel continued holding her hair, but found himself pushing her head deeper, his hips thrusting more forcefully into her mouth as he lost his inhibitions.

"Yes, Dolly." He found himself moaning, "Keep going, don't stop." He felt as if he'd lost his mind, his body completely overriding his senses, overriding every rational thought he could try and muster.

He could feel the slightly familiar sensation of build up occurring, his mind feeling increasingly desperate - *no*. It couldn't end now, not like this.

He pulled her head away. He could see the wetness dripping from the corner of lips, he moved a hand to her mouth, wiping it away with his thumb. He could feel his manhood throbbing, aching for more. He looked around the room, his mind searching for the next thing to do to satiate the hunger in his groin.

"Lay over there." The words came out huskier, more forceful than he had intended. He was flooded with new emotions, new hormones. He could feel them surging through him, primal urges surging through his blood. He had never felt so alive, so raw, *so desperate.*

He watched as she walked away, her ass swaying side to side as she did so before taking a seat on the edge of his desk. She perched upon it, leaning back on her elbows again.

He felt himself at attention, his body drawn to hers, ready to become one. Ready to come together. His mouth felt dry, but no matter, he would soon wet his lips on Dolly.

He strode over to her, his mind awash with lust so strong he swore he could smell it in the air.

As he approached, Dolly laid down, stretching her arms above her head. Swallowing, Samuel took hold of her hands, holding them in his own, before pulling her wrists together, her palms pressed against each other as if in prayer. He looked up the length of her arms, her fingers pointing to the crucifix on the wall behind them.

*Don't look at it.*

He focussed his eyes on the blonde, becoming totally intoxicated with the sight of her. This was heaven on earth, this is what the gospels wrote of, she was the song of songs. He leant down, placing a delicate kiss on her lips.

"Who do you belong to?"

"You, Father." She smiled, her eyes bright and playful as Samuel positioned himself at her entrance for the first time.

This was it. He was really going to do it.

He could feel the wetness of her, warm against his tip. He could feel the heat from her sucking him in, He pushed the head of his shaft ever so slightly in. He felt the hot pressure ensnare him. It was inviting, homely even.

He pushed the tip further in, his senses melting away as he sunk deeper and deeper into her. He felt his breath catch in his throat, a low groan bubbling at the base of his neck, escaping through gritted teeth. Dolly laid perfectly still, her hands still bound by his own as he pushed himself in to the hilt.

He opened his eyes, his heart beating out of his chest. He looked into the glistening green eyes and he felt the beats skip. He leant down, capturing her mouth in his own.

"You okay?" The gentle face came from below him. He nodded wordlessly. As he did so, Dolly raised her legs and wrapped them around his waist, her heels digging in slightly on his hip bone, pulling him further towards her.

He thought he couldn't be any deeper until she squeezed her thighs around him, pulling him in to the base. He could feel the skin of his pubis against hers, feel the soft skin caressing his own.

He gasped.

This was it.

He was no longer a virgin.

Whatever happened next would happen...

But the 'worst' was over.

He buried his mouth in the crook of her neck, determined to hide the tears that began to pool in his eyes. He gently began to pull out, the blonde arching her hips away from him as he did so and in a fraction of a second he was almost out of her, the breeze on his shaft. Without warning, she curved her hips towards him and pulling him in again. He felt the contraction, the heat...

He felt his own mind empty.

There was nothing else.

Nothing but her.

This moment couldn't end.

It was perfect.

"Oh F-father..." She whispered, her voice high with lust, "Is this your first time?" He pulled away and looked at her - was it really so obvious? "Like, totally don't worry if it is, it's still good! I'm just super excited to be your first!"

He nodded dumbly.

"Like, you can go faster, it won't hurt me..." She paused, biting her lip, "Or maybe it will a little, but I'll like it."

Samuel felt like his brain broke. He could barely focus on her words with the other sensations building in his groin, in his chest. His mind had lost all processing power and the comprehension of words was scarcely going to be prioritized. Dolly looked at his dark, blank eyes and twisted her face as she thought for a moment,

"Harder, Daddy!" She beamed.

Harder? The word made it through, sharp like a knife slicing through the mist. He thrust again and she moaned. He pulled out to the tip and slammed again,

"Yes! That's it! Keep going!" She spoke breathily through the thrusts, which came harder and faster now. Samuel could feel some primal instinct taking over, his mind foggy with Dolly as the only beacon.

*Harder.*

*Faster.*

*More.*

*More.*

*Keep going.*

*Please...*

*Please.*

He felt as she wrapped around him even tighter, and he struggled to balance whilst gripping her hands. He released her so that he was able to support himself and her newly freed fingers found their way to his back.

He moaned in new found pleasure as her nails scratched at his skin, the sharp bite drawing blood, the broken skin prickling with delight.

*Perhaps this was the penance?*

*No.*

*It felt too good.*

He thrust into her again and again, their bodies mangled together in a chimera of limbs, bound by sweat and saliva. His lips found hers again, the sweet taste of her mouth, their tongues dancing together as fire erupted between them.

He could feel the pressure building.

No.

*No.*

He did not want this to end.

*He could not let this end.*

He needed to keep going. Forever. For eternity.

In this perfect world where she was his and he was hers and there was no one else and never would be.

He could feel the end nearing, feel the surge coursing through his body. He felt Dolly shudder beneath him, moans and gasps escaping from her perfect mouth. He felt like the earth and heavens were moving around him as his mind wiped itself of all thoughts and for one blissful second the world stopped.

It was euphoric.

He felt himself stagger within her as he came, hard and fast, goosebumps sprinting along his skin and his hairs stood at attention.

He could feel the energy draining quickly from him as he moaned her name loudly.

*Praise be unto Dolly.*

He could worship at the shrine of her forever.

He could come and lay his feeble tribute inside of her, in hope of this glorious rapture again and again and again.

*He would pray for it.*

*He would beg for it.*

*He would be beholden to her forever more.*

He pulled out slowly. Their combined fluids spilled out onto the desk.

*If a man has a seminal emission, he shall bathe all his body in water and be unclean until evening. As for any garment or any leather on which there is seminal emission, it shall be washed with water and be unclean until evening.*

He watched as Dolly shuffled backwards, swinging her legs over the desk and stretching effortlessly, a sleepy look in her eyes.

"That was super fun." She hopped from her perch and swayed over to him. "How are you feeling?"

How was he feeling? *How was he feeling?*

His legs were trembling. He was unsure how he had found the strength to stand.

His heart was pounding. He felt like a heart attack was imminent.

His blood was both hot and cold.

His mind had been a blissful, euphoric blank and was now flooding with the realization and clarity of everything he had just done.

And the revelation that he would do it again.

And again.

*And again.*

He would do it as long as she would let him. His hunger for her had not been satiated. The bread and fish for 5000 people would not feed the pit of yearning he now possessed.

No.

A beast has been awoken and it was loud and carnivorous and ferocious.

How had he kept himself under control all of these years? How had he been so *good?* Had he always been missing out on *this?* Was this what everyone else enjoyed?

He understood it now.

This was the real reason men went to war.

The reason they'd search for a chalice of immortal life.

To be forever young.

It would be to worship a goddess like Dolly, and to have her grant the nectar of pleasure.

To hell with Hell.

He would suffer an eternity of torture to have her.

He would let the devil burn him, whip him, torment him if it meant that Dolly would do the same in his lifetime.

He wanted to beg for her to please him, and he wanted to please her.

He wanted to touch her ass, plunge his *dick* into her and hear her scream his name whilst he sang her praises.

"Father? Are you ok?" He felt the gentle touch on his shoulder, her delicate fingers upon his flesh. He looked into her eyes, grabbed her by the scruff of her hair and kissed her firmly. He felt their teeth catch as he deepened the kiss, her tongue pushing back against his own as he held her close, desperate to taste all that he could in the moment, savoring every morsel of her that he could. He pulled his mouth less than a millimeter from hers,

"You will be mine and no others. You are mine." He almost purred the words as he pushed his lips back onto the gasping blonde who did nothing to push him away. Instead she pulled one of his hands from her waist and to her breast.

"Yes, Father." She said between gasps, willing him to continue. He took her ample breast in his hand, kneading it softly. He could not give this up. Now that he had started, he knew this was the path for him.

He would keep Dolly his dirty little secret. She would be his and he hers.

*Forever.*

They pulled apart, breathless and with bruised lips.

"Do you want me to go, Father?" Her voice sounded almost pleading. He swallowed, drinking in her flushed pink skin. He shook his head,

"The only place you're going is with me." A moment of surprise flashed across Dolly's features, "Really?"

"Really." He nodded, stroking a lock of her hair between his finger and thumb. "You are mine. God brought you here, and I have made the decision that I cannot let you go. You need *looking after.*" His eyes darkened, "You are wayward and promiscuous. You are Mary Magdalene unbound. But I shall have you and I shall *tame* you and you *will* be mine."

Dolly gasped, her plump lips falling open, "But you said…"

"It doesn't matter what I said before." He let his hand fall from her breast to her wet pussy…*God it felt so good to say it.* He grabbed her with his palm, his finger teasing around her clit, "You asked me to help you. *Control you.*" He slid his middle finger inside her, where moments ago his dick had been, "And…" He bit the lobe of her ear, his hot breath against her skin, "I intend to follow through with that promise. You *will not* have sex *without my permission.*" His fingers teased her more, "*You will not have sex without me.*" He purred. "Think of these as your *commandments. And like God…I will punish you if you sin.*"

Dolly quivered under his touch. "Y-yes."

"Yes, what?" He felt a fire burning in the pit of his stomach. He felt so alive. So raw and real.

"Yes, F-Father." She stumbled over the words as his hand entered her again, his thumb encircling her clit, adding gentle amounts of pressure. He kept his other hand firmly in her hair, controlling her head, stopping her from moving away, not that she tried.

"Good girl." The words came out like a growl. He hadn't intended it but it felt so good. So right. "Now... remind me...what are the rules..."

"I-I will not take part in any sex acts...with..."

"Good girl, keep going..."

"With myself...or...or *anyone* else..." Her voice was husky and distracted. He pushed harder against her clit,

"With *anyone* other than *me.*"

"With anyone other than you." She half opened her eyes to meet his lustful gaze.

"Keep going." He lightened the pressure on his thumb, circling the throbbing organ again as the wetness around his fingers grew,

"I will not show any-anyone my body..."

"Except..." His voice a warning tone,

"Except for you."

"Good girl."

"That was all of them..." Samuel paused.

"You will pleasure *me* and only *me.*" She smiled, her voice bright as she said the words,

"I will pleasure you...and only you..." As she finished the sentence, she reached around to his ass, squeezing it gently.

"You will always do as I command."

"I will do as you command." He thought for a moment.

"And like a good Christian... you will start every session, on your knees, *praying.*"

"What should I pray for?"

"For me. Pray that I will allow you to come for me. That I will make you scream God's name as I bury myself inside you. Pray that you will always serve me, and I shall serve you." He felt his chest heave. Had he gone too far? That sounded too much. He'd just compared himself to

God.

Well, perhaps tonight wasn't the night for following rules, after all, he'd just about broken every promise he'd ever made to himself. There were very few covenants left unshattered.

"Samuel..." Dolly murmured. He felt a shiver run down his spine, his nerves twanging with a cold chill. It felt so poetic when she said his name. "Fuck me please. Fuck me again." He groaned, biting at her neck,

"Pray for me, Dolly. Pray."

"Please Daddy." She dropped to her knees, his fingers falling from her pussy as she did so. "Please Daddy, make me come again." She placed her hands together in prayer at his feet, kneeling. He looked down on her, her tits perfectly smushed together by her arms, her thighs soft and supple, her messy hair falling over her shoulders, and her eyes...

Her huge sea-green eyes that looked up at him with such earnest want.

"Good girl." He patted the top of her head. He realized that in his yearning and weakness, he had forgotten his own inexperience. "Tell me, Dolly. How should I make you come?"

"Fuck me, Father. Please."

"And how should I fuck you, my child?" Dolly grinned widely at the first time really hearing the Priest swear. She looked around the room for inspiration.

"Can we fuck in the church, Father?"

Samuel thought for a moment. Surely not? That was a step too far. Anyone could see. That would be too much... too brave.

He glanced at the clock on the wall.

8pm.

Not many people came to church on weekdays at

8pm.

He could lock up for the night.

He could have her anywhere he wanted.

Anywhere *she* wanted.

In God's own house.

He snorted inwardly. He'd never fucked when his parents were home like many boys in high school had - perhaps fucking in the house of God was like that...he was *everyone's* father after all. Right? He took a steadying breath as he took her hand, helping her to her feet.

"I must lock the doors." He tried to sound somber as he looked for his shirt and pants that were strewn in a corner. As he bent down, Dolly tapped his shoulder and held out some white fabric.

"This is easy to throw on, right?"

# XII.

He looked at the garment in her hands. His Alb. A symbol of purity and sanctity. He should not wear it ever again. He could not wear it.

He wasn't pure.

He felt his gaze wander over the nude woman before him, his erection stirring.

*Screw that.*

He took the robes from her and threw them on. It felt oddly satisfying to be naked under one of his most sacred costumes.

He swept his hands through his hair a few times, tidying it up as best he could, before heading to the main doors. He stuck his head out of the door, peering around into the sunset sky before pulling the doors closed.

He pulled the key from the little drawer near the entrance and locked it shut. He walked around the back, checking the doors to the office and the emergency exit that had been installed some 30 years ago.

Everything was secure.

And thank God for that. He found himself standing at the head of the altar, staring at the beautiful glass windows, the sunlight streaming through casting rainbow patterns on the carpet.

He turned around and saw Dolly, completely nude, walking up the aisle towards him.

He had called her perfect before.

The Venus.

In his mind he had seen her as a goddess and pure heaven.

But now?

Now he did not have the words to describe her.

He could not possibly put meaning to the way her pale skin glistened under the hue of the glass. Fractured glimmers of rich tones highlighting her skin like an oil painting. Every soft curve lit up with delicate, golden lighting. Her hair around her shoulders, falling onto her breasts which hung heavily on her chest, her hips swaying with every step. Her skin unblemished, unmarked like an immaculate creation.

His mind could hardly comprehend it. No words could ever do it justice.

The memory of it, would never do it justice.

He approached her slowly, taking gentle gliding steps. He cupped her cheeks in his hands, her eyes full of awe and wonder. It wouldn't matter how often he replayed this in his mind, how many times he would try to conjure images of celestial beings or exotic places - nothing, *nothing* would compare to her right now. He beheld her, his angel, his heaven.

*Therefore what God has joined together, let no one separate.*

He caressed down her neck, to her shoulders, watching as she turned her face into his palm, kissing it softly.

"I belong to no one but you." She whispered. Samuel felt everything swell within him, an almighty knot in his stomach, twisting down to his groin and stirring awake his cock under his Alb.

His hands stroked down her waist, under her ass and between her legs.

"Where did you want to be taken?" He asked her, his voice firm, betraying a hint of nervousness. She looked around as if seeing the room for the first time. The cold stone walls and warm glass windows. The threadbare carpet down the aisle and the ornate altar at the front. The confessional box, wooden and traditional and the pews and the wooden pulpit. She pointed slowly.

"Up there. I think that would be fun!" Samuel followed the line of her finger to the pulpit, raised above all else. It wasn't a large space, but it would feel secluded and special within the majesty of the grand building. He nodded. Taking her by the hand and leading her up the little steps. They could hardly fit together and certainly not laying down. He pulled her close, kissing at the nape of her neck as she looked out over the pews and altar, her face illuminated softly by the fading sunlight streaming in.

She pushed him gently down onto his knees and then onto his butt. He looked up at her in all of her splendor, the contours and curves of her body, the view nothing short of divine. He would never want the image removed from his memory. Not when he was worn and gray, not when he was burning in the deepest pit of hell. It would comfort him for whatever eternity lay ahead for him.

Dolly knelt opposite him, her body close and knees between his own legs. Her delicate fingers felt up the inside of his calf, of his thigh, making their way to the hidden erection beneath the Alb. *Some purity.*

He felt her hands reach his dick and slowly move up and down, painfully calm, controlled. He gasped, closing his eyes, the warmth building up in his groin and spreading like wildfire through his stomach and into his chest. He could feel the familiar warmth caress his brain, the wonderful fog enveloping him, a fog that he'd still not broken free of from their last session. He moaned softly, as her fingers kept working him,

"Good girl, but if you keep going like that, I won't be able to fuck you like you asked."

*Dance, then, wherever you may be...*

She pushed the Alb up and over his waist, exposing himself to her again. His fingers reached between her legs, feeling the familiar wetness, the sticky nectar on his fingers. He slid them over her, spreading her apart before bringing the digits to his own mouth. He sucked them gently, tasting the salty-sweet liquid, closing his eyes in a low grunt as he did so. He would lead her and she would follow,

*I am the Lord of the Dance, said he.*
*And I'll lead you all wherever you may be...*

He pulled her closer as she kneeled astride him, positioning himself under her, ready to receive her. He squeezed her flesh firmly, tilting his head as he willed her down on top of him.

He felt the blaze of her heat as she sunk down, his blood boiling with the intense fire of his passion for her. How had anyone ever convinced him that virginity and chastity was the way of God? He had lived in such fear, in such denial of everything that is beautiful...

*I danced on a Friday and the sky turned black;*
*It's hard to dance with the devil on your back...*

He pulled her forcefully down onto him again and again, the Alb bunching up his back as he thrust into her, his vision starry as he did so, her figure silhouetted in the light, the pleasure on her face barely visible. She whispered his name, *Father*, over and over as she bounced on him, her breasts swaying and oscillating with the increasing rigor of his thrusts. As he became faster and faster she buried her hands in her own hair, pulling it from her face as she called out for him to go *harder* and *faster* and the words scratched that wild animal in his head, his bones responding to the instruction, pounding her harder and harder.

He could feel himself sweating through the white fabric, the material clinging to his wet skin. Dolly reached down and hastily pulled it over his head, tossing it over the little balcony of the pulpit. He wrapped his arms around her, before slapping her ass hard as she rode him, groaning at the pleasure the sound gave him. He pulled out of her quickly, before using his legs to flip her onto her stomach and without warning, burying himself inside her again, her peachy ass on full display, ready to hit again and again. He muttered things about her being a naughty girl and tempting priests, slapping her ass, whipping her with his fingers as he did so with every thrust, her pale flesh blooming in pink marks that caused her to moan and whimper with delight...

*They whipped and they stripped and they hung me high;*

He pummeled into her again and again, sheer ecstasy overwhelming him, his grunts and groans no longer suppressed, no longer buried deep in his insecurities or innocence. He needed this, and he had filled the void that had been missing from him for so long. He felt complete, he felt whole. He felt *Dolly.*

He could feel the blonde's growing tightness as she clamped and rocked back and forth, his dick buried deep within her. He could feel his own release imminent and looming, but he wasn't ready, not yet. He reached around her, his fingers expertly finding her clit, the blonde shuddering beneath him, impressed at how well his memory had mapped out her body.

His fingers danced over it, again and again, moving her flesh aside to garner more access as he continued the vigorous onslaught from behind.

He felt wild.

The moans pouring from her lips were only sending him further into his insane abyss.

But he didn't care. This was everything.

There was nothing else.

He thrust again. Her throbbing clit under his fingers, her throbbing pussy around his pulsing cock.

His heart raced with the thrill, the excitement, the lust.

He could feel her legs beginning to tremble under the power of his movements, her fingers and toes curling as she screamed out in euphoria again and again, almost convulsing with joy...

*And I'll lead you all wherever you may be,*
*And I'll lead you all in the dance, said he...*

He thrust into her again, feeling the pressure that had grown within him burst out. He felt himself shudder as she came, his fingers gripping her pink skin, squeezing as he braced himself through his release. He stammered out a final groan as he collapsed on top of her. Their sweaty bodies in a messy pile in the tiny wooden space.

*I'll live in you if you'll live in me...*

After a few moments to catch his breath he pulled away steadily, leaning himself back against the cold wood to gather his thoughts. He picked up the Alb and cleaned the back of her legs before cleaning himself. At least it came in use - though its sanctity was fully tarnished. She leant back against him, nestling herself in his chest.

He could feel her beating heart, the warmth of her skin and the gentle rhythm of her breathing.

He stroked her hair softly, closing his eyes.

He couldn't give this up if he tried.

Nor would he want to.

He took control of his own breathing, inhaling her scent. The musty church and ancient air.

She couldn't leave. Not now. Not ever.

"Stay with me." He whispered. She nodded sleepily as she adjusted to fit into his arms. She curled her legs up and looked up at him with a sleepy smile.

"Yes, Father."

"Stay with me, *always.*"

"I belong to you, and no one else, Father." She giggled slightly as she said it.

"And I belong to you. And no one else, Dolly." He whispered, stroking her hair.

They fell asleep there, intertwined, nude like the first people, embraced and emboldened.

\*\*\*

Samuel would later reflect on that day in years to come, remembering it as the first time he really began to know God, and what experiences humans were meant to experience in their lifetime. For the first time, so many of the songs and quotes made sense on a fundamental level, on a *human* level. For all of their flaws and misdemeanors.

For all of their euphoric highs and abysmal lows. For all of the triumph and suffering.

For everything he could experience.

He had experienced *living.*

He had experienced *her.*

*I am the Lord of the Dance, said he.*

END

# UNTITLED

Printed in Great Britain
by Amazon